KT-169-520

Donovan's Big Day

C334016320

Donovan's Big Day

by Lesléa Newman

Illustrations by Mike Dutton

TRICYCLE PRESS
Berkeley

Text copyright © 2011 by Lesléa Newman
Illustrations copyright © 2011 by Mike Dutton

All rights reserved.
Published in the United States by Tricycle Press,
an imprint of Random House Children's Books,
a division of Random House, Inc., New York.
www.randomhouse.com/kids

Tricycle Press and the Tricycle Press colophon are
registered trademarks of Random House, Inc.

Library of Congress Cataloging-in-Publication Data
Newman, Lesléa.
  Donovan's big day / by Lesléa Newman ;
illustrations by Mike Dutton. — 1st ed.
     p. cm.
  Summary: From the moment Donovan wakes in the
morning, he painstakingly prepares for his special
 role in the wedding ceremony of his two mothers.
 [1. Stories in rhyme. 2. Lesbian mothers—
Fiction. 3. Weddings—Fiction. 4. Mothers
and sons—Fiction. 5. Families—Fiction.]
I. Dutton, Mike, ill. II. Title.
  PZ8.3.N4655Don 2011
  [E]—dc22
                    2009048488

ISBN 978-1-58246-332-2 (hardcover)
ISBN 978-1-58246-392-6 (Gibraltar lib. bdg.)

Printed in China

Design by Chloe Rawlins
Typeset in Advert and Franklin Gothic
The illustrations in this book were rendered
in gouache with digital finish.

3 4 5 6 — 18 17 16 15

First Edition

For Mary Grace Newman Vazquez
happily ever after

—L. N.

For Alex and all the songs she sings to me

—M. D.

When Donovan opened his eyes in the morning
he remembered that it was a very BIG day
and he had a very BIG job to do.

But first . . .

He had to tumble out of bed
the minute Grandpa woke him up
and not turn over and shut his eyes
or hide his head under the blankets
or go back to sleep
for even just five more minutes.

He had to race downstairs
and give Sheba her breakfast
and gobble up all the pancakes
that Grandma served him
and slurp down all the juice
that Grandpa poured him
and not drop his fork or spill his syrup
or make any kind of fuss.

He had to rush back upstairs and wash his hands
and clean his nails and scrub his face
and brush his teeth and rinse his mouth
and comb his hair and not leave the bathroom
a great big mess with water splashed everywhere
and dirty towels all over the floor.

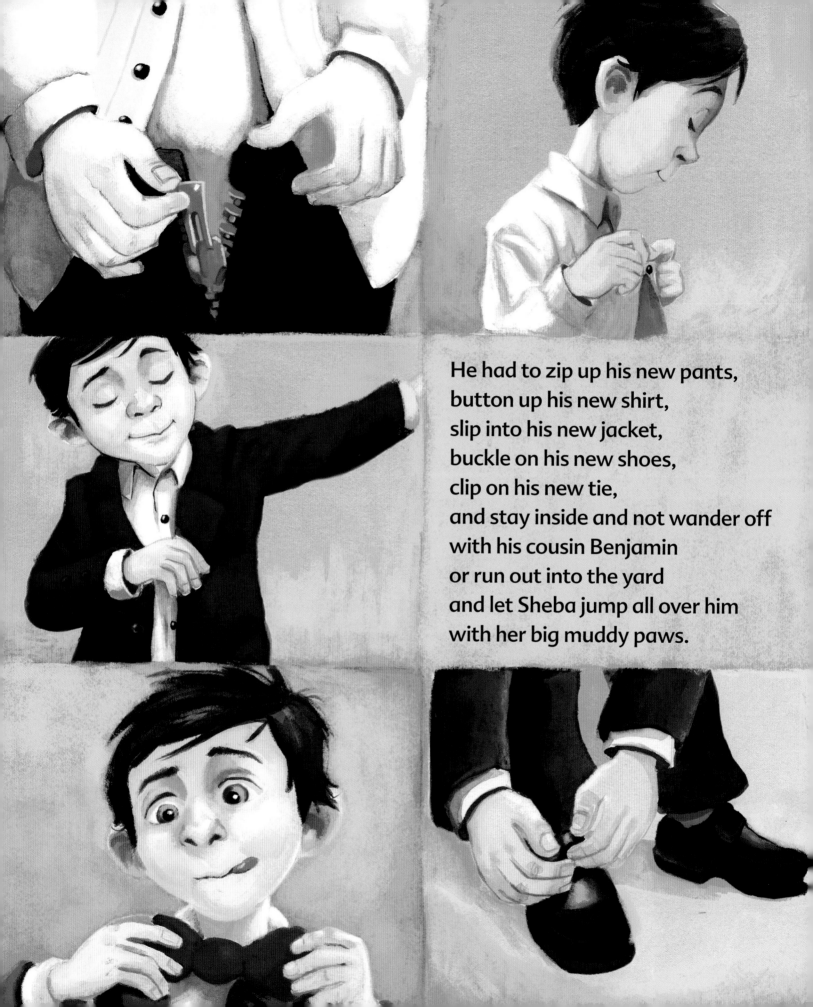

He had to zip up his new pants,
button up his new shirt,
slip into his new jacket,
buckle on his new shoes,
clip on his new tie,
and stay inside and not wander off
with his cousin Benjamin
or run out into the yard
and let Sheba jump all over him
with her big muddy paws.

He had to tuck the little white satin box
that Aunt Jennifer gave him
into his inside jacket pocket
and keep track of it at all times
and not shake it or crush it
or squash it or lose it
no matter what.

He had to fly outside the minute
he heard Uncle Gregory honk the horn
and climb into the big backseat
of Uncle Gregory's shiny blue car
and squeeze in next to his cousins
and sit absolutely still
without kicking his feet
so his new clothes wouldn't wrinkle
and his new shoes wouldn't scuff.

He had to be the first one to hop off his seat,
scramble out of the car,
scurry up some steep steps,

hurry through a large, sunlit lobby,

and dash into a loud, crowded room
full of hundreds of grown-ups
all dressed up in their very best clothes
and he had to say hello
to every single one of them
while they shook his hand,
gave him a hug,
kissed his cheek,
and told him how very handsome
he looked on this very BIG day.

He had to take his place
with Grandma and Grandpa
and Nana and Poppa
right behind his baby cousin Sienna
who had flowers in her hair
and flowers on her dress
and flowers in a basket
looped over her arm
and after he waited and waited and waited and waited . . .

He had to walk—

not run, not skip, not hop, not leap, not bounce, not dance—

down the aisle.

He had to stand very very quietly
and not tap his feet or fidget
while one grown-up read a poem

and another grown-up played the piano

and another grown-up sang a song . . .

Until Aunt Jennifer told him it was time
and then Donovan reached
into his inside jacket pocket
and took out the little white satin box
he had been keeping there
and held it in his hand.

He opened the box very carefully.
He handed one shiny gold ring to Mommy.
He handed one shiny gold ring to Mama.
He stood next to both of them
without saying a word
while they slid the shiny gold rings
onto each other's fingers,
looked into each other's eyes,
said mushy things to each other,
and smiled and laughed and cried.

When the tall grown-up in the long black robe said,
"I now pronounce you wife and wife,"
Donovan threw his arms around his mothers
while everyone clapped their hands
and stamped their feet
and whooped and whistled
and hollered, "Hooray!"

And then after everyone grew quiet
Donovan remembered
there was one more very BIG job
for him to do:

"You may now kiss the brides."